W9-AOE-858

DISCARD

Ollie the Stomper

Olivier Dunrea

HOUGHTON MIFFLIN HARCOURT
Boston   New York

For Mack

To access the read-along audio file, visit
WWW.HMHBOOKS.COM/FREEDOWNLOADS
ACCESS CODE: STOMP

AGES	GRADES	GUIDED READING LEVEL	READING RECOVERY LEVEL	LEXILE® LEVEL
4–6	P–1	E	7–8	270L

The text of this book is set in Shannon.
The illustrations are ink and watercolor on paper.

The Library of Congress Cataloging-in-Publication Data is on file.

ISBN: 978-0-618-33930-3 hardcover
ISBN: 978-0-618-75504-2 board book
ISBN: 978-0-544-14715-7 paper-over-board reader
ISBN: 978-0-544-14676-1 paperback reader

Manufactured in China
SCP 10 9 8 7 6 5 4 3 2 1
4500448167

This is Ollie.

This is Gossie. This is Gertie.

They are goslings.

Gossie wears bright red boots.

Gertie wears bright blue boots.

Ollie wants boots.

Gossie and Gertie tromp
in the straw.

Ollie stomps after them.

Gossie and Gertie romp
in the rain.

Ollie stomps after them.

Gossie and Gertie jump
over a puddle.

Ollie stomps after them.

Gossie and Gertie march
to the pond.

Ollie stomps after them.

Gossie and Gertie hide
in the pumpkins.

"I want boots!" Ollie shouts.

Gossie and Gertie
stomp to Ollie.

Gossie gives Ollie a red boot.

Gertie gives Ollie a blue boot.

Ollie hops to the barn.

Gossie and Gertie follow.

Ollie stomps to the piggery.

Gossie and Gertie follow.

Ollie stares at his boots.

"These boots are too hot!"
Ollie shouts.

Ollie kicks off his boots.

Gossie kicks off her boot.
Gertie kicks off her boot.

"Let's go swimming!" Ollie shouts.
And they do.